Alexandria Public Library
P.O. Box 67
Alexandria, OH 43001-0067

WITHDRAWN

Team Spirit

THE DALLAS MAVERICKS

BY
MARK STEWART

Content Consultant
Matt Zeysing
Historian and Archivist
The Naismith Memorial Basketball Hall of Fame

CHICAGO, ILLINOIS

Norwood House Press
P.O. Box 316598
Chicago, Illinois 60631

For information regarding Norwood House Press, please visit our website at: www.norwoodhousepress.com or call 866-565-2900.

All photos courtesy of AP Images—AP/Wide World Photos, Inc. except the following:
Topps, Inc. (6, 14, 20, 21 bottom, 34 right, 37 & 43);
Star Company (34 left); Author's collection (40).
Special thanks to Topps, Inc.

Editor: Mike Kennedy
Designer: Ron Jaffe
Project Management: Black Book Partners, LLC.
Special thanks to Merri Lynne Alexander

Library of Congress Cataloging-in-Publication Data

Stewart, Mark, 1960-
 The Dallas Mavericks / by Mark Stewart ; with content consultant Matt Zeysing.
   p. cm. -- (Team spirit)
 Summary: "Presents the history, accomplishments and key personalities of the Dallas Mavericks basketball team. Includes timelines, quotes, maps, glossary and websites"--Provided by publisher.
 Includes bibliographical references and index.
 ISBN-13: 978-1-59953-067-3 (library edition : alk. paper)
 ISBN-10: 1-59953-067-8 (library edition : alk. paper)
 1. Dallas Mavericks (Basketball team)--History--Juvenile literature. I. Zeysing, Matt. II. Title. III. Series: Stewart, Mark, 1960- Team spirit.
 GV885.52.D34S74 2007
 796.323'64097642812--dc22
                                                2006015334

© 2007 by Norwood House Press.
All rights reserved.
No part of this book may be reproduced without written permission from the publisher.

The Dallas Mavericks is a registered trademark of Dallas Basketball Limited.
This publication is not affiliated with the Dallas Mavericks, Dallas Basketball Limited, The National Basketball Association or The National Basketball Players Association.

Manufactured in the United States of America.

COVER PHOTO: Dirk Nowitzki and Josh Howard "high five" over Darrell Armstrong during the 2005 playoffs.

Table of Contents

CHAPTER	PAGE
Meet the Mavericks	4
Way Back When	6
The Team Today	10
Home Court	12
Dressed For Success	14
We Won!	16
Go-To Guys	20
On the Sidelines	24
One Great Day	26
Legend Has It	28
It Really Happened	30
Team Spirit	32
Timeline	34
Fun Facts	36
Talking Hoops	38
For the Record	40
Pinpoints	42
Play Ball	44
Glossary	46
Places to Go	47
Index	48

SPORTS WORDS & VOCABULARY WORDS: In this book, you will find many words that are new to you. You may also see familiar words used in new ways. The glossary on page 46 gives the meanings of basketball words, as well as "everyday" words that have special basketball meanings. These words appear in **bold type** throughout the book. The glossary on page 47 gives the meanings of vocabulary words that are not related to basketball. They appear in ***bold italic type*** throughout the book.

BASKETBALL SEASONS: Because each basketball season begins late in one year and ends early in the next, seasons are not named after years. Instead, they are written out as two years separated by a dash, for example 1944–45 or 2005–06.

Meet the Mavericks

There are many ways to win a basketball game. The Dallas Mavericks have proved this over the years. They have won with tough, hard-working players who dive for loose balls and out-hustle the other team's superstars. They have won with smooth, elegant athletes who swish jump shots and glide through the air for slam dunks. And they have won with some very unusual players whose skills are not so easy to describe.

Basketball fans never know what kind of team the Mavericks will put on the floor from season to season. However, they do know this—the "Mavs" will score a lot of points, make a lot of plays, and win a lot of games.

This book tells the story of the Mavericks. They are an exciting team to root for, and an interesting team to watch. From the owner of the team all the way down to the last man on the bench, the Mavericks are focused on doing whatever it takes to outscore their opponents—and make basketball fun!

Dirk Nowitzki gives Devin Harris a friendly head tap after a great play.

Way Back When

In the 1970s, Texas was a "football state" and Dallas was a "football town." Two wealthy business leaders, Donald Carter and Norm Sonju, believed there was room in the city for a **professional basketball** team. Sports fans in Dallas had not supported basketball in the past, but the **National Basketball Association (NBA)** was beginning an exciting new *era*, and Carter and Sonju decided it was worth another try.

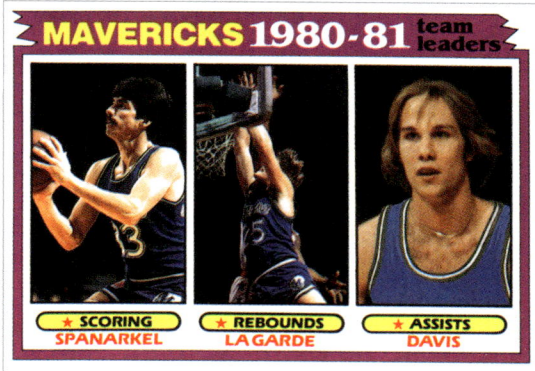

The Mavericks joined the NBA for the 1980–81 season. Their first stars were Brad Davis, Tom LaGarde, and Jim Spanarkel, and they were coached by Dick Motta. The Mavericks won only 15 games that year, but the following season three talented young players joined the team—Mark Aguirre, Jay Vincent, and Rolando Blackman. By 1983–84, Dallas had a very *competitive* team, and made it to the **playoffs**.

The Mavericks added more good players to their **lineup** during the 1980s, including Derek Harper, Sam Perkins, Roy Tarpley, James Donaldson, and Detlef Schrempf. In 1986–87, they finished

ABOVE: Jim Spanarkel, Tom LaGarde, and Brad Davis were the leaders of the Mavericks in their first season.

RIGHT: Mark Aguirre slices past A.C. Green and Kareem Abdul-Jabbar of the Los Angeles Lakers. **BELOW**: Brad Davis looks for an open teammate.

first in the **Midwest Division**. One year later they made it all the way to the **Western Conference** Finals. It took seven *grueling* games for the Los Angeles Lakers to defeat them.

As the stars of the 1980s became old or injured, or were traded away, the Mavericks found it very difficult to replace them. In 1991–92, Dallas won only 22 games. During the next two seasons, the Mavericks won a total of just 23! The bright side of this story was that the team's poor record meant it would get high picks in the **draft**. The Mavericks used those picks to select young stars Jim Jackson, Jamal Mashburn, and Jason Kidd. They were known around the NBA as the "Three J's." They were fun to watch, but Dallas continued to struggle.

Things began to change after Don Nelson was hired to coach the Mavericks. He built a new team around three *different* young stars—Steve Nash, Michael Finley, and Dirk Nowitzki. Nelson was one of the first NBA coaches to realize how to blend the talents of players from different countries. The Mavericks had European players, South American players, African players, and Asian players in their lineup. It only took a couple of years for them to become one of the NBA's best teams again.

During the 1999–00 season, a man named Mark Cuban bought the Mavericks. Cuban ran a computer software company, but his first love was basketball. He promised the fans of Dallas that he would do everything he could to bring them their first championship. Since then, the Mavericks have been one of the most fun teams in the NBA to watch.

LEFT: Dirk Nowitzki drives against Shawn Marion of the Phoenix Suns. **TOP**: Steve Nash throws up a left-handed layup against the Sacramento Kings.

The Team Today

The Mavericks are one sports team that actually lives up to its name. A maverick is a *range animal* that runs apart from the herd. The Mavericks are part of the NBA, but they do not play the game the way other teams do. Sometimes Dallas puts five small, fast players on the court. Sometimes they use a lineup of big rebounders and rugged defenders.

In 2004, the team traded its **All-Star point guard**, Steve Nash, and hired a former point guard, Avery Johnson, to coach the team. The offense was no longer run by a "little man." Instead, the Mavericks put the ball in the hands of seven-footer Dirk Nowitzki—and surrounded him with smart, creative **role players** like Josh Howard, Jerry Stackhouse, and Jason Terry.

Team owner Mark Cuban encourages the Mavericks to be different. He made millions of dollars in business this way, and he believes being true mavericks gives his team its best chance to win a championship.

Dirk Nowitzki offers some friendly words of encouragement to a smiling Josh Howard.

Home Court

The Mavericks play their home games in the American Airlines Center. Some fans call it the "AAC," but most call it the "Hangar." It opened in 2001, and it is also the home of the Dallas Stars of the **National Hockey League (NHL)**.

The first thing you notice about the arena are the huge arches at the main entrance. Inside this beautiful building, there are special *retractable* seats that move forward for basketball games and pull back for hockey games. Something fans cannot see are the large, comfortable locker rooms. The players love them.

The Hangar also has three-sided shot clocks, so everyone in the arena knows how much time is left to shoot. Owner Mark Cuban ordered these clocks made when a fan pointed out that not everyone could see the old one-sided ones.

AMERICAN AIRLINES CENTER BY THE NUMBERS
- The arena has 19,200 seats for basketball.
- The arena cost $420 million to build.
- The arena has won more than a dozen awards for its **innovative** design.
- The arena has an art collection worth $3 million.

Josh Howard scores against the San Antonio Spurs in the American Airlines Center.

Dressed for Success

The Mavericks' team colors are silver, white, and two shades of blue. When the team started, its colors were bright blue and green. They still wear special uniforms with these old colors from time to time. The Mavericks tried red and silver uniforms for a few games during 2003–04, but the fans liked their other colors better.

The team *logo* has also changed over the years. It used to be a capital M "wearing" a cowboy hat, inside a basketball. Today, the Dallas logo is a stylish horse set against a blue basketball. To show their team spirit, all of the Mavericks sometimes wear the same kind of headbands, or the same long socks.

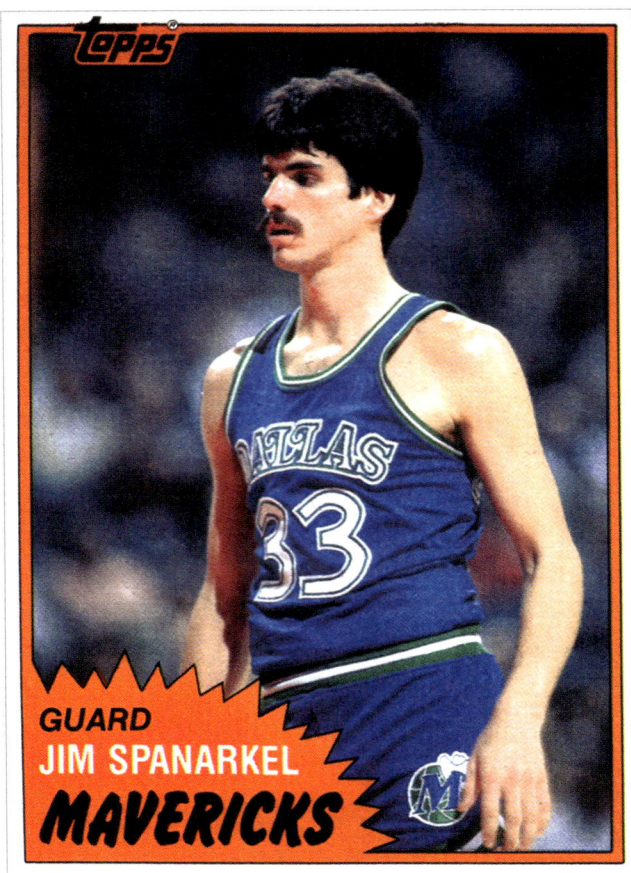

Jim Spanarkel wears the blue-white-and-green road uniform of the 1981 Dallas Mavericks.

UNIFORM BASICS

The basketball uniform is very simple. It consists of a roomy top and baggy shorts.

- The top hangs from the shoulders, with big "scoops" for the arms and neck. This style has not changed much over the years.

- Shorts, however, have changed a lot. They used to be very short, so players could move their legs freely. In the last 20 years, shorts have actually gotten longer and much baggier.

Basketball uniforms look the same as they did long ago…until you look very closely. In the old days, the shorts had belts and buckles. The tops were made of a thick cotton called "jersey," which got very heavy when players sweated. Later, uniforms were made of shiny **satin**. They may have looked great, but they did not "breathe." Players got very hot! Today, most uniforms are made of **synthetic** materials that soak up sweat and keep the body cool.

Jason Terry wears the Mavericks' home white uniform during a 2006 game.

We Won!

The Mavericks played their first 25 seasons in the NBA with one goal—to reach the **NBA Finals**. Every time they had a team good enough to play for the championship, however, someone else in the Western Conference was just a little bit better. In 1988,

they played a thrilling series against the Los Angeles Lakers in the Western Conference Finals. Neither team lost a home game, but the Lakers had an extra game on their court in Los Angeles, and won four games to three. In 2003, the Mavericks put up a good fight against the San Antonio Spurs, but lost the Western Conference Finals in six games.

Finally, in 2005–06, the team had everything it needed to "Win the West." Mark Cuban and Don Nelson put together a group of talented and hard-working players, and coach Avery Johnson taught them that they had to do more than just score baskets to win—they had to play tough defense 48 minutes a game.

ABOVE: Erick Dampier blocks the shot of Memphis star Pau Gasol during the first round of the 2006 playoffs. **RIGHT**: Jason Terry and DeSagana Diop give Tim Duncan no room to maneuver during their 2006 series with the Spurs.

The Dallas lineup was excellent. Jason Terry, the team's point guard, attacked the defense at all times. So did Jerry Stackhouse, who played both guard and forward. Josh Howard, known mostly as a defensive star, showed he could score, too. This meant that the team's best player, Dirk Nowitzki, did not have to have a great game in order for the Mavericks to win.

As the season went on, others on the Mavericks began to play important roles in the team's victories, including center Erick Dampier, forwards Adrian Griffin and Keith Van Horn, and guards Marquis Daniels and Devin Harris. The Mavericks finished the year with a record of 60–22. Only San Antonio had more wins.

After beating the Memphis Grizzlies in the first round of the playoffs, the Mavericks faced the Spurs. Dallas fans still remembered the loss to San Antonio in 2003, and wanted to prove they were the better team. After six exciting games, the teams were tied 3–3. In the fourth quarter of Game Seven—which was played on San Antonio's home court—Nowitzki made a difficult shot with time running out to tie the score, and the Mavericks went on to win in overtime, 119–111.

Now only the Phoenix Suns stood between Dallas and its first trip to the NBA Finals. The Suns were led by Steve Nash, who had once been a star for the Mavericks. It was strange to see their old friend in another uniform, but that is just life in the NBA.

The Suns played well, but could not stop Nowitzki. With the series tied 2–2, he scored 50 points in Game Five to give Dallas an important victory. Everyone was saying what a great player the team had in Nowitzki, but he reminded everyone that he was merely part of a great team. The Mavericks proved this in Game Six, when the Suns shot their way to a big lead in the first quarter.

In the old days, Dallas would have simply tried to outscore its opponent in order to catch up. These new Mavericks caught up by playing incredible defense—then scored 40 points in the fourth quarter to finish off the Suns 102–93. After a quarter-century of coming close, the Mavericks were finally crowned Western Conference champions!

ABOVE: Old friend and ex-teammate Steve Nash congratulates Dirk Nowitzki on reaching the NBA Finals.   **RIGHT**: Nowitzki battles Shaquille O'Neal of the Heat during the 2006 NBA Finals.

The team's wonderful season ended in the NBA Finals. They were able to win their first two games against the Miami Heat, but lost the next four. Miami's Dwyane Wade and Shaquille O'Neal were just too hard to handle. The players and fans in Dallas were heartbroken, but also proud of their accomplishment. They vowed to work even harder to return for another try.

Go-To Guys

To be a true star in the NBA, you need more than a great shot. You have to be a "go-to guy"—someone teammates trust to make the winning play when the seconds are ticking away in a big game. Mavericks fans have had a lot to cheer about over the years, including these great stars…

THE PIONEERS

BRAD DAVIS — 6' 3" Guard

- Born: 12/17/1955
- Played for Team: 1980–81 to 1991–92

Brad Davis was unwanted by every other team in the NBA. When the Mavericks gave him a chance, he quickly became their leader.

MARK AGUIRRE — 6' 6" Forward

- Born: 12/10/1959
- Played for Team: 1981–82 to 1988–89

Mark Aguirre was the first player picked in the 1981 NBA Draft. He used his wide body and quick moves to get open shots, and he could shoot from anywhere on the court. Aguirre **averaged** 25 points or more for the Mavericks in four different seasons.

ROLANDO BLACKMAN   6' 6" Guard

- BORN: 2/26/1959
- PLAYED FOR TEAM: 1981–82 TO 1991–92

The last man Dallas opponents wanted to see with the ball in his hands and the clock running down was Rolando Blackman. He had one of the best outside shots in basketball.

DEREK HARPER   6' 4" Guard

- BORN: 10/13/1961   • PLAYED FOR TEAM: 1983–84 TO 1993–94 & 1996–97

Derek Harper was no fun to guard. If a defender played him tight, he could dribble around him. If he gave Harper too much room, he could shoot over him. If two men guarded him, Harper would whip the ball to an open teammate.

SAM PERKINS   6' 9" Forward

- BORN: 6/14/1961
- PLAYED FOR TEAM: 1984–85 TO 1989–90

At one time or another, Sam Perkins played all five positions for the Mavericks. He had all the moves on offense, while his long arms and leaping ability made him an excellent defender.

LEFT: Mark Aguirre
TOP: Rolando Blackman   **ABOVE**: Sam Perkins

MODERN STARS

JIM JACKSON   6' 6" Guard/Forward

- BORN: 10/14/1970
- PLAYED FOR TEAM: 1992–93 TO 1996–97

Jim Jackson had a "nose" for the basket—when he sensed that he could score, there was no stopping him. Jackson once averaged over 25 points a game for the Mavericks.

JAMAL MASHBURN
6' 8" Forward

- BORN: 11/29/1972
- PLAYED FOR TEAM: 1993–94 TO 1996–97

Jamal Mashburn was on his way to becoming the NBA's next superstar when an injured knee slowed him down. Even playing in pain, "Monster Mash" could be a scary player.

MICHAEL FINLEY   6' 7" Guard/Forward

- BORN: 3/6/1973
- PLAYED FOR TEAM: 1996–97 TO 2004–05

Michael Finley gave the Mavericks good shooting and great defense during his years with the team. Dallas could always count on him to be on the court—he led the NBA in minutes played three times.

ABOVE: Jamal Mashburn, Jason Kidd, and Jim Jackson—the "Three J's."
TOP RIGHT: Dirk Nowitzki   **BOTTOM RIGHT**: Josh Howard

DIRK NOWITZKI 7' 0" Forward

- BORN: 6/19/1978
- FIRST SEASON WITH TEAM: 1998–99

Dirk Nowitzki grew up in Germany, and learned to play basketball thinking he would be a guard. He combined these skills with the height of a center to become one of the hardest men in the NBA to guard.

STEVE NASH 6' 3" Guard

- BORN: 2/7/1974
- PLAYED FOR TEAM: 1998–99 TO 2003–04

Very few people believed Steve Nash could be a starting player in the NBA. After he came to the Mavericks, he proved he could be that and more. Nash made the All-Star team twice while playing for Dallas.

JOSH HOWARD 6' 7" Forward

- BORN: 4/28/1980
- FIRST SEASON WITH TEAM: 2003–04

When every team but the Mavericks passed up a chance to draft Josh Howard, he decided he would make the NBA pay. He did this by becoming the team's best attacking player—on defense, on offense, and under the backboards.

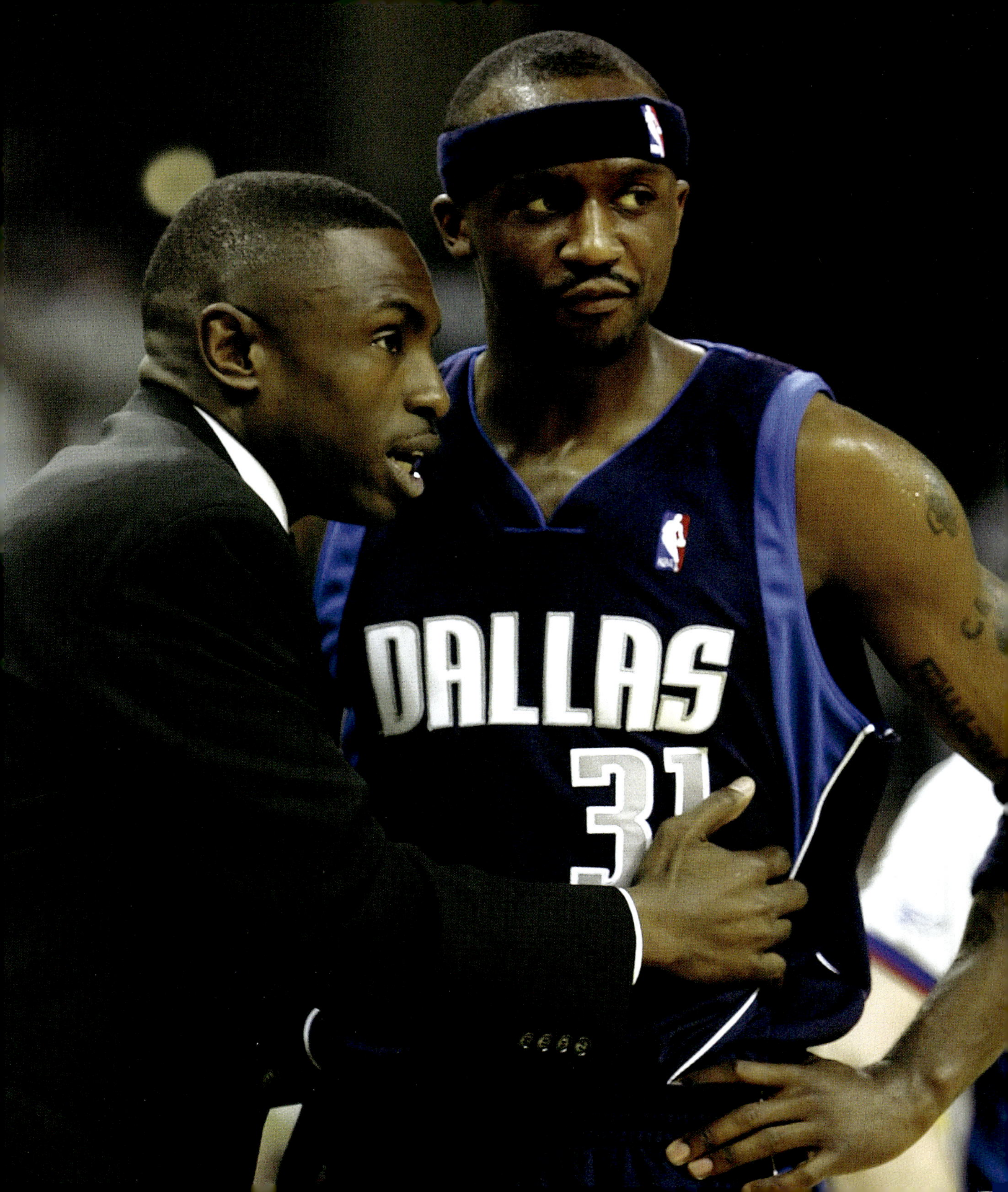
DALLAS
31

On the Sidelines

For most of their history, the Mavericks have been at their best when they have an experienced coach on the sidelines. Their first coach was Dick Motta. He joined the team just three years after leading the Washington Bullets to the NBA championship. Motta made a game plan for his players, and promised that they would win if they followed it. In no time, the Mavericks became a playoff **contender**.

Don Nelson took over the team during the 1997–98 season. His teams, The Milwaukee Bucks and the Golden State Warriors, had won 50 or more games nine times. After rebuilding the Mavericks, Nelson turned them into a 50-win team.

In 2005, Nelson handed the team over to his assistant, Avery Johnson. Johnson had no coaching experience, but he had a special connection with the players. Johnson had been a player himself for the Mavericks just two years earlier. He did such a good job in his first full season that he was named NBA Coach of the Year!

Avery Johnson talks things over with point guard Jason Terry. Johnson played the point for the Mavericks a few years earlier.

One Great Day

FEBRUARY 18, 2006

Players who stand seven feet tall are not supposed to be great outside shooters. And they certainly are not supposed to win the NBA's 3-Point Shootout! Apparently, no one ever bothered to tell this to Dirk Nowitzki.

Nowitzki did not follow the same path to the NBA as other All-Stars. He grew up in Germany, where he learned a different style of basketball. In Europe, everyone is expected to be able to dribble, pass, play defense, and shoot—no matter how tall they are or what position they play.

From an early age, Nowitzki had a special skill for shooting. He thought he would be a guard until he got too tall. He thought he would be a forward until he kept growing. When Nowitzki finally stopped, he was the only center on the planet that could swish 25-foot jump shots.

Nowitzki was invited to compete in the 3-Point Shootout in 2000, and finished second. A year later, he came in third. In 2006, however, it looked like he would not make it past the first round. He made a shot with no time left on the clock to stay alive, then began to heat up in the next round.

By the time the final round began, Nowitzki was on fire. He nailed eight of his first ten shots, and the crowd rose to its feet and began to roar. He made seven more to finish with 18 points—a number too good for the other finalists, Gilbert Arenas and Ray Allen, to beat.

When reporters asked Nowitzki if he liked shooting 3-pointers without a defender's hand in his face, he smiled and said, "That's my kind of game!"

LEFT: Dirk Nowitzki takes aim during the 2006 3-Point Shootout.
ABOVE: Nowitzki shows off his trophy as Shootout champion.

Legend Has It

Which team was the victim of the Mavericks' greatest comeback?

LEGEND HAS IT that it was Michael Jordan and the 1997–98 Chicago Bulls. With less than four minutes to play, the Mavericks were behind by 15 points. Suddenly, everyone on the team began making shots. Dallas tied the game in the final seconds, and then won it in overtime 104–97. The Bulls, who would win the NBA championship later that year, finished the season with a record of 62–20. The Mavericks finished 20–62.

ABOVE: Michael Jordan scores against the Mavericks.
RIGHT: Shawn Bradley towers over one of his fans.

Was center Shawn Bradley too tall to live in a regular house?

LEGEND HAS IT that he was. NBA players often have to have special beds, furniture, and countertops made for them. Shawn Bradley—who stood 7' 6"—had to have a special *house*. His Dallas home had extra-tall doors and an extra-tall shower, as well as a bed that was nine feet long.

Did the Mavericks find their all-time favorite player in Alaska?

LEGEND HAS IT that they did—and that they almost "lost" him! Brad Davis, who wore a Dallas uniform for twelve years, was playing for the Anchorage Northern Knights of the minor-league **Continental Basketball Association (CBA)** in 1980. He had tried to make it in the NBA, but was **cut** by three different teams. When the Mavericks first offered Davis a job, he told them he would rather finish the year in Anchorage and then go back to the University of Maryland. Later, Davis decided to give the NBA one more try. That year he led Dallas in **assists** and tied the team record for points in a game.

It Really Happened

NBA coaches spend a lot of time yelling at referees. It is part of their job. Sometimes they really *are* mad at the officials, and sometimes they are just pretending. Fans love it when their coach gets mad at a referee. They think he is fighting for the team. No one knew *what* to think, however, during a game between the Mavericks and Utah Jazz in 1984.

During a timeout, a famous mascot called The Chicken ran onto the court to entertain the fans. He began dancing to a song called "Whip It" and started to twirl a rag dummy dressed as a referee. Dallas coach Dick Motta—who was famous for his battles with the men in stripes—decided to have some fun. Motta ran over to The Chicken, grabbed the dummy, and pretended to beat it up. The players watched with open mouths. The crowd went wild.

"The fans loved it," said Ted Giannoulas, the man inside The Chicken suit. "The Dallas players were screaming for their coach to kick it again."

How did the officials feel about Motta's crazy behavior? Referee Jim Wishmier was standing on the sidelines and laughing so hard he had to put a towel over his face. As soon as the song ended, Motta walked back to the bench—and received a standing ovation.

Dick Motta loved to give the referees a hard time.

Team Spirit

The Mavericks have some of the loudest, craziest fans in basketball. When the Mavericks played in Reunion Arena, these fans were called the "Reunion Rowdies." The louder they got, the better the team seemed to play. Once, for an important playoff game in Seattle, owner Mark Cuban actually bought tickets for any fan who was willing to fly to the city and root for the Mavericks. Today, they get to scream for the team in the Mavericks' new arena.

Cuban is the most famous sports fan in Dallas. He wants everyone to love the "Mavs" as much as he does. He jumps out of his seat after great plays, raises his arms on 3-point shots, and yells advice to the players from his seat behind the bench. When the Mavericks win, he jumps for joy.

Although Cuban does not consider himself a "cheerleader," he likes the fact that the fans get excited when he does. As he sees it, if the team's owner is having fun at games, why shouldn't they?

Mark Cuban leads the cheers at Mavericks games.

Timeline

The basketball season is played from October through June. That means each season takes place at the end of one year and the beginning of the next. In this timeline, the accomplishments of the Mavericks are shown by season.

1980–81
The Mavericks join the NBA.

1983–84
Mark Aguirre leads the Mavericks to the playoffs for the first time.

1986–87
The Mavericks win 50 games for the first time.

1994–95
Jason Kidd is named NBA Co-**Rookie of the Year**.

1996–97
Shawn Bradley leads the NBA with 3.4 blocked shots per game.

Mark Aguirre

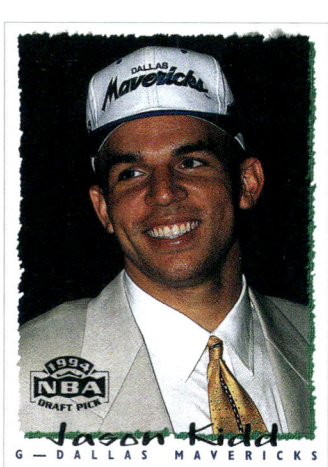

Jason Kidd

Michael Finley

Dirk Nowitzki

2000–01
Michael Finley leads the NBA with 3,443 minutes played.

2004–05
Dirk Nowitzki becomes the first Maverick to be named First-Team **All-NBA**.

1999–00
Hubert Davis leads the NBA in 3-point shooting.

2002–03
The Mavericks set a new team record with 60 wins.

2005–06
The Mavericks reach the NBA Finals for the first time.

Hubert Davis

Jerry Stackhouse slams one during the 2006 playoffs.

Fun Facts

RAP IT UP
The Mavericks sometimes wear special green uniforms. They were designed by hip-hop superstar Sean "P Diddy" Combs.

THREES ARE WILD
During a game in March of 2005, Michael Finley made all eight of his 3-point shots.

ALMOST PERFECT
The Mavericks started the 2002–03 season by winning their first 14 games in a row. They fell one win short of the NBA record of 15.

ABOVE: Sean "P Diddy" Combs   **RIGHT**: Detlef Schrempf

GERMAN IMPORTS

Dirk Nowitzki was not the first German star for the Mavericks. In 1985–86, Detlef Schrempf and Uwe Blab both suited up for the team.

THE BENEFACTOR

Mark Cuban once hosted a television show called *The Benefactor*. He gave away $1,000,000 to the winner of the game.

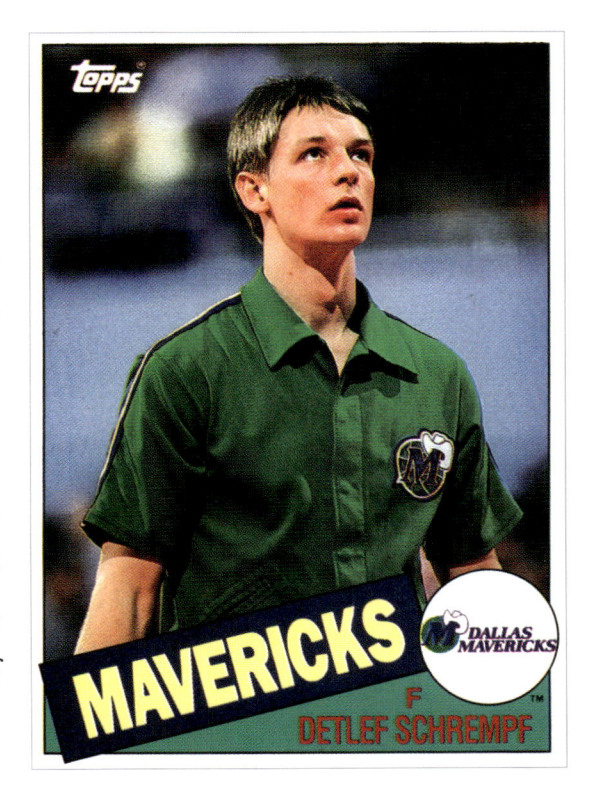

OVERSEAS SENSATION

Wang Zhi-Zhi, the team's backup center in 2001–02, was the NBA's first Asian-born player. He was born in Beijing, China.

IN GOOD COMPANY

When Dirk Nowitzki scored 50 points against the Suns in the 2006 Western Conference Finals, he became only the eighth forward in the history of the playoffs to accomplish this feat.

Talking Hoops

"I was looking for something that was challenging and fun. Living in Dallas and being a Mavs season-ticket holder, what could be more of a challenge than turning around a **franchise** that hadn't been to the playoffs in 10 years?"

—Owner Mark Cuban, on why he bought the team

"I've always found that the more **versatile** players I have, the better off I am."

—Don Nelson, on why he always looked for players who could play more than one position

"We are a team that succeeds when we hustle."

—Avery Johnson, on the key to winning for the Mavericks

ABOVE: Don Nelson and Mark Cuban
RIGHT: Josh Howard gives his wristband to a happy fan.

"We know we must play 'D' to go far in the playoffs, so I try to set an example."

—*Josh Howard, on being a team leader*

"I'm a true believer that work pays off."

—*Michael Finley, on his philosophy as an NBA player*

"I don't think we have an MVP, but we have a great team with a lot of great players. We're doing this as a team—playing defense as a team, offense like a team."

—*Dirk Nowitzki, on why he does not consider himself the team MVP*

For the Record

The great Mavericks teams and players have left their marks on the record books. These are the "best of the best"…

MAVERICKS AWARD WINNERS

WINNER	AWARD	SEASON
Roy Tarpley	NBA Sixth Man Award	1987–88
Jason Kidd	Co-Rookie of the Year	1994–95
Dirk Nowitzki	3-Point Shootout Champion	2005–06
Avery Johnson	Coach of the Year	2005–06

MAVERICKS ACHIEVEMENTS

ACHIEVEMENT	SEASON
Midwest Division Champions	1986–87
Midwest Division Champions	2005–06
Western Conference Champions	2005–06

TOP: Coach of the Year Avery Johnson
BOTTOM: A souvenir pennant from the team's first year.
RIGHT: Jason Kidd, who shared the Rookie of the Year award with Grant Hill of the Detroit Pistons.

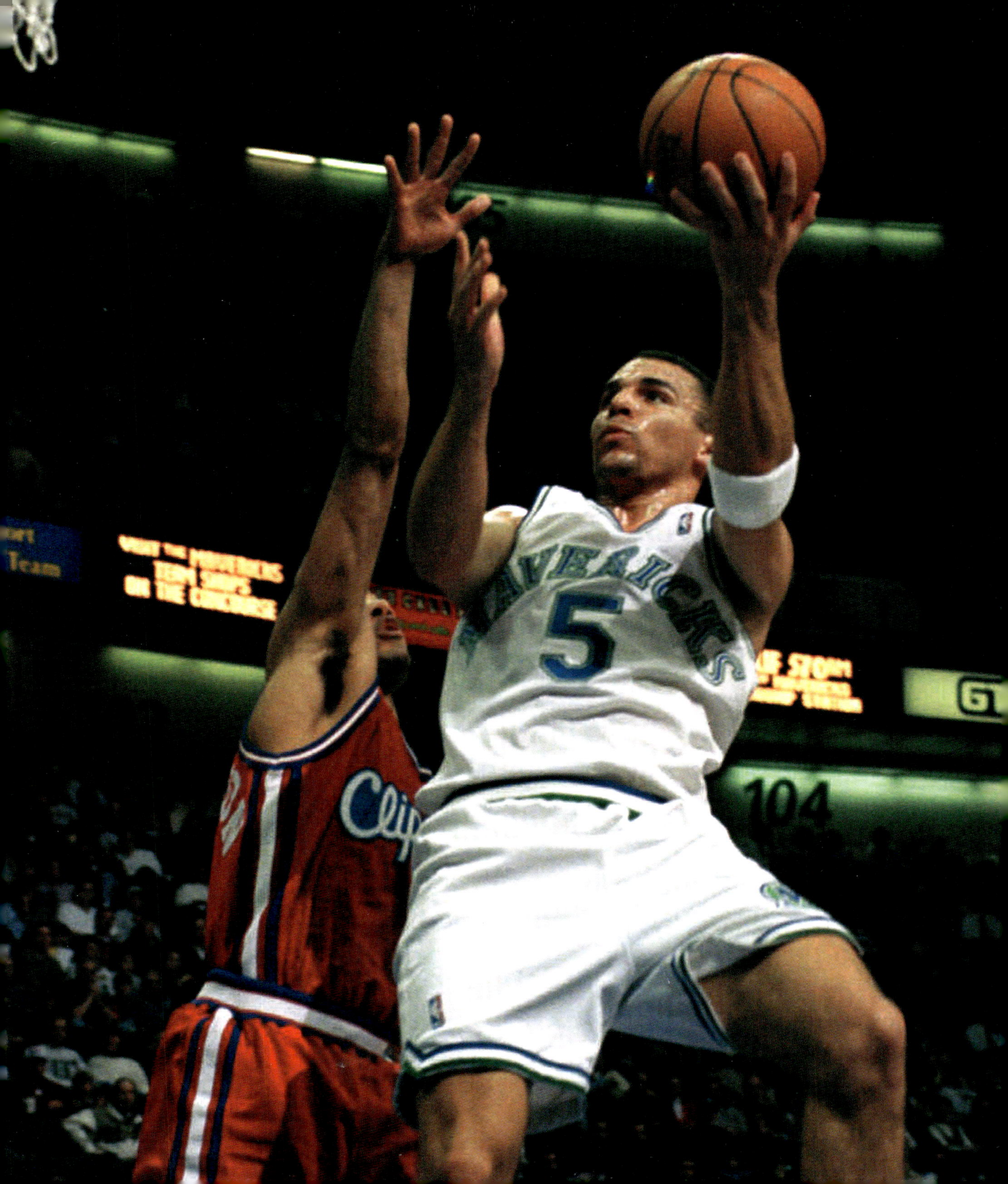
5
104

Pinpoints

The history of a basketball team is made up of many smaller stories. These stories take place all over the map—not just in the city a team calls "home." Match the push-pins on these maps to the Team Facts and you will begin to see the story of the Mavericks unfold!

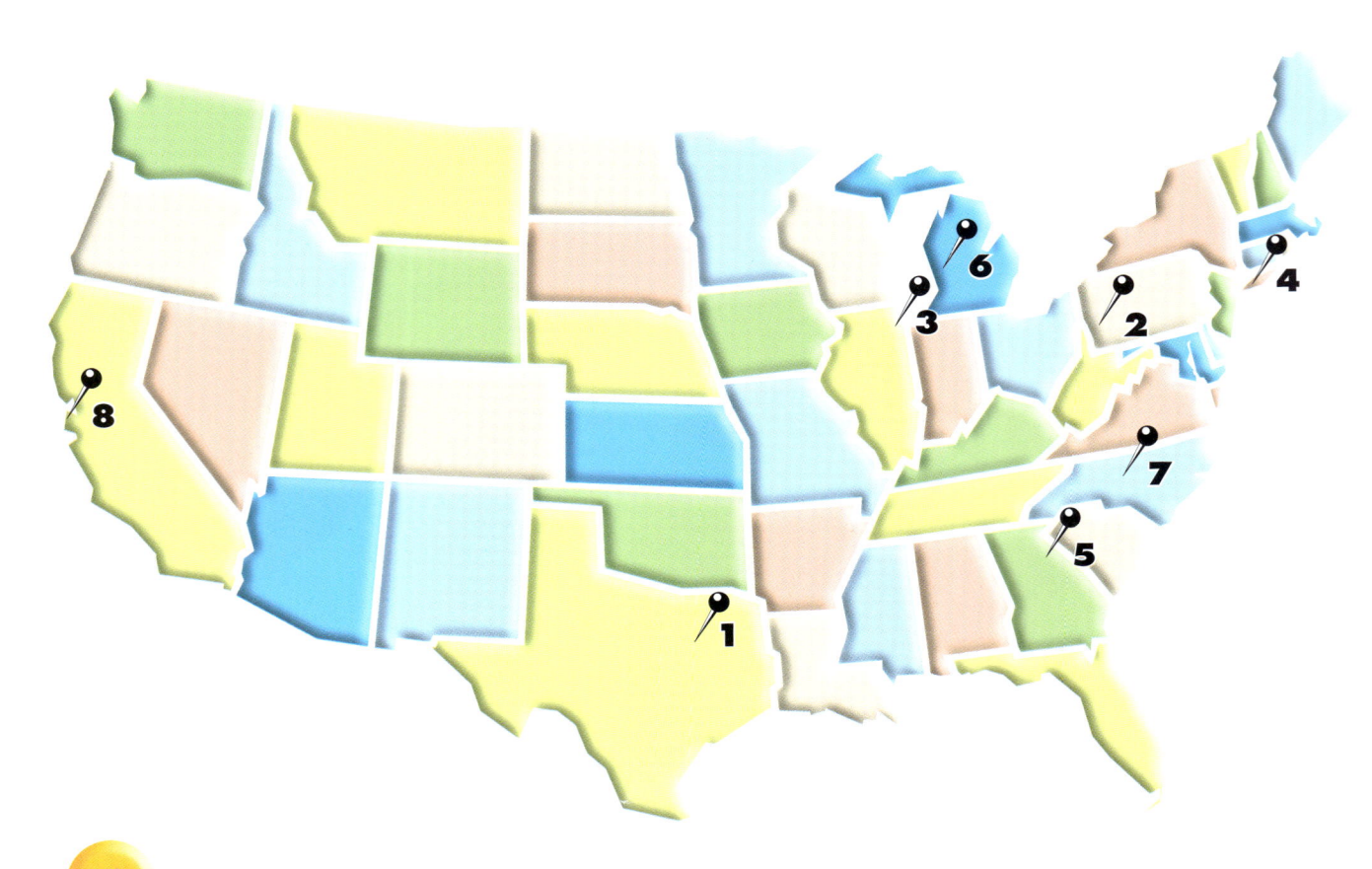

TEAM FACTS

1. Dallas, Texas—*The Mavs play here.*
2. Pittsburgh, Pennsylvania—*Mark Cuban was born here.*
3. Chicago, Illinois—*Mark Aguirre was born here.*
4. Brooklyn, New York—*Sam Perkins was born here.*
5. Elberton, Georgia—*Derek Harper was born here.*
6. Muskegon, Michigan—*Don Nelson was born here.*
7. Winston-Salem, North Carolina— *Josh Howard was born here.*
8. San Francisco, California—*Jason Kidd was born here.*
9. Johannesburg, South Africa—*Steve Nash was born here.*
10. Panama City, Panama—*Rolando Blackman was born here.*
11. Wurzburg, Germany—*Dirk Nowitzki was born here.*
12. Beijing, China—*Wang Zhi-Zhi was born here.*

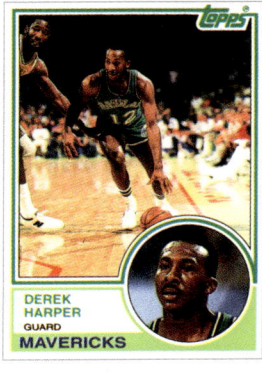

Derek Harper

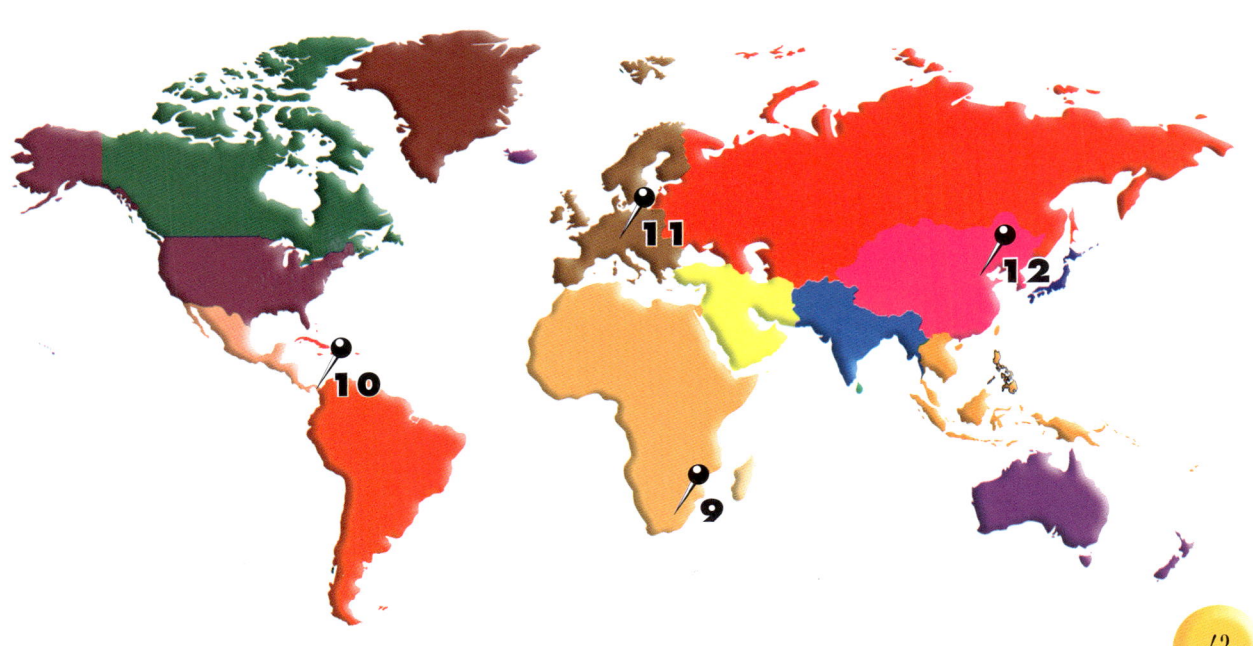

Play Ball

Basketball is a sport played by two teams of five players. NBA games have four 12-minute quarters—48 minutes in all—and the team that scores the most points when time has run out is the winner. Most baskets count for two points. Players who make shots from beyond the three-point line receive an extra point. Baskets made from the free-throw line count for one point. Free throws are penalty shots awarded to a team, usually after an opponent has committed a foul. A foul is called when one player makes hard contact with another.

Players can move around all they want, but the player with the ball cannot. He must bounce the ball with one hand or the other (but never both) in order to go from one part of the court to another. As long as he keeps "dribbling," he can keep moving.

In the NBA, teams must attempt a shot every 24 seconds, so there is little time to waste. The job of the defense is to make it as difficult as possible to take a good shot—and to grab the ball if the other team shoots and misses.

This may sound simple, but anyone who has played the game knows that basketball can be very complicated. Every player on the court has a job to do. Different players have different strengths and weaknesses. The coach must mix these players in just the right way, and teach them to work together as one.

The more you play and watch basketball, the more "little things" you are likely to notice. The next time you are at a game, look for these plays:

PLAY LIST

ALLEY-OOP—A play where the passer throws the ball just to the side of the rim—so a teammate can catch it and dunk in one motion.

BACK-DOOR PLAY—A play where the passer waits for his teammate to fake the defender away from the basket—then throws him the ball when he cuts back toward the basket.

KICK-OUT—A play where the ball-handler waits for the defense to surround him—then quickly passes to a teammate who is open for an outside shot. The ball is not really kicked in this play; the term comes from the action of pinball machines.

NO-LOOK PASS—A play where the passer fools a defender (with his eyes) into covering one teammate—then suddenly passes to another without looking.

PICK-AND-ROLL—A play where one teammate blocks or "picks off" another's defender with his body—then cuts to the basket for a pass in the confusion.

Glossary

BASKETBALL WORDS TO KNOW

ALL-NBA—An honor given to the NBA's best players at the end of the season. The "first team" is made up of the best player at each of the five positions.

ALL-STAR—Someone selected to play in the NBA's annual All-Star Game.

ASSISTS—Passes that lead to baskets.

AVERAGED—Made an average of.

CONTENDER—A team good enough to play for the championship.

CONTINENTAL BASKETBALL ASSOCIATION (CBA)—A professional league that uses players who are not good enough or not yet ready for the NBA.

CUT—Taken off the team.

DRAFT—The meeting each year at which NBA teams take turns choosing the best amateur and foreign players.

FRANCHISE—One of many teams that are "partners" in the same league.

LINEUP—The main players on a basketball team.

MIDWEST DIVISION—A group of teams, located in the Midwest, that makes up one of the divisions of the NBA.

NATIONAL BASKETBALL ASSOCIATION (NBA)—The professional league that has been operating since 1946–47.

NATIONAL HOCKEY LEAGUE (NHL)—The professional hockey league that has been in operation since 1917.

NBA FINALS—The playoff series that decides the championship of the league.

PLAYOFFS—The games played after the regular season to determine which teams make it to the NBA Finals.

POINT GUARD—The player whose job it is to guide the team on the court and start plays on offense.

PROFESSIONAL BASKETBALL—Basketball played for money. College and high school players are not paid, so they are considered "amateurs." Professional players are sometimes called "pros."

ROLE PLAYERS—People who are asked to do specific things when they are in a game.

ROOKIE OF THE YEAR—An award given to the best first-year player, or "rookie." When the vote for the award is a tie, two players are named Co-Rookies of the Year.

WESTERN CONFERENCE—One of two groups of teams that make up the NBA. The winner of the Western Conference Finals plays the winner of the Eastern Conference Finals for the NBA championship.

OTHER WORDS TO KNOW

COMPETITIVE—Good enough to win.

ERA—A period of time in history.

GRUELING—Extremely tiring or difficult.

INNOVATIVE—Done in a new way.

LOGO—A symbol or design that represents a business or team.

RANGE ANIMAL—A horse or cow that is free to roam the open range.

RETRACTABLE—Able to be pulled back.

SATIN—A smooth, shiny fabric.

SYNTHETIC—Made in a laboratory, not in nature.

VERSATILE—Able to do many things well.

Places to Go

ON THE ROAD

AMERICAN AIRLINES CENTER
2500 Victory Avenue
Dallas, Texas 75219
(214) 747-6287

NAISMITH MEMORIAL BASKETBALL HALL OF FAME
1000 West Columbus Avenue
Springfield, Massachusetts 01105
(877) 4HOOPLA

ON THE WEB

THE NATIONAL BASKETBALL ASSOCIATION   www.nba.com
- *to learn more about the league's teams, players, and history*

THE DALLAS MAVERICKS   www.nba.com/mavericks
- *to learn more about the Dallas Mavericks*

THE BASKETBALL HALL OF FAME   www.hoophall.com
- *to learn more about history's greatest players*

ON THE BOOKSHELF

To learn more about the sport of basketball, look for these books at your library or bookstore:

- Hareas, John. *Basketball.* New York, NY: DK, 2005.
- Hughes, Morgan. *Basketball.* Vero Beach, FL: Rourke Publishing, 2005.
- Thomas, Keltie. *How Basketball Works.* Berkeley, CA: Maple Tree Press, distributed through Publishers Group West, 2005.

Index

PAGE NUMBERS IN **BOLD** REFER TO ILLUSTRATIONS.

Abdul-Jabbar, Kareem	7
Aguirre, Mark	6, 7, 20, **20**, 34, **34**, 43
Allen, Ray	27
American Airlines Center	**12**, 13
Arenas, Gilbert	27
Blab, Uwe	37
Blackman, Rolando	6, 21, **21**, 43
Bradley, Shawn	29, **29**, 34
Carter, Donald	6
Combs, Sean "P Diddy"	36, **36**
Cuban, Mark	9, 11, 13, 16, **32**, 33, **33**, 37, 38, **38**, 43
Dampier, Erick	**16**, 17
Daniels, Marquis	17
Davis, Brad	6, **6**, 7, 20, 29
Davis, Hubert	35, **35**
Diop, DeSagana	17
Donaldson, James	6
Duncan, Tim	17
Finley, Michael	9, 22, 35, **35**, 36, 39, 43, **43**
Gasol, Pau	16
Giannoulas, Ted	30
Green, A.C.	7
Griffin, Adrian	17
Harper, Derek	6, 20, 43, **43**
Harris, Devin	**4**, 17
Hill, Grant	40
Howard, Josh	**10**, 11, **12**, 23, **23**, 39, **39**, 43
Jackson, Jim	7, 22, **22**
Johnson, Avery	11, 16, **24**, 25, 38, 40, **40**
Jordan, Michael	28, **28**
Kidd, Jason	7, **22**, 34, **34**, 40, **41**, 43
LaGarde, Tom	6, **6**
Marion, Shawn	**8**
Mashburn, Jamal	7, 22, **22**
Motta, Dick	6, 25, 30, **31**
Nash, Steve	9, **9**, 11, 18, **18**, 23, 43
Nelson, Don	9, 16, 25, 38, **38**, 43
Nowitzki, Dirk	4, 8, 9, **10**, 11, 17, 18, **18**, 19, **19**, 23, **23**, 26, **26**, 27, **27**, 35, **35**, 37, 39, 40, 43
O'Neal, Shaquille	19, **19**
Perkins, Sam	6, 21, **21**, 43
Schrempf, Detlef	6, 37, **37**
Sonju, Norm	6
Spanarkel, Jim	6, **6**, 14
Stackhouse, Jerry	11, **35**
Tarpley, Roy	6, 40
Terry, Jason	11, 17, **17**, 15, 24
Van Horn, Keith	17
Vincent, Jay	6
Wade, Dwyane	19
Wishmier, Jim	30
Zhi-Zhi, Wang	37, 43

The Team

MARK STEWART has written more than 20 books on basketball, and over 100 sports books for kids. He grew up in New York City during the 1960s rooting for the Knicks and Nets, and now takes his two daughters, Mariah and Rachel, to watch them play. Mark comes from a family of writers. His grandfather was Sunday Editor of *The New York Times* and his mother was Articles Editor of *The Ladies Home Journal* and *McCall's*. Mark has profiled hundreds of athletes over the last 20 years. He has also written several books about his native New York, and New Jersey, his home today. Mark is a graduate of Duke University, with a degree in history. He lives with his daughters and wife, Sarah, overlooking Sandy Hook, NJ.

MATT ZEYSING is the resident historian at the Basketball Hall of Fame in Springfield, Massachusetts. His research interests include the origins of the game of basketball, the development of professional basketball in the first half of the twentieth century, and the culture and meaning of basketball in American society.

JUN -- 2007

J 796.323 Ste

WITHDRAWN